A *magical sound*

No sooner was she outside on the street than
Minnie suddenly found that she could hear all sorts
of voices with her green ear, voices she could not
hear with the ordinary pink one. She could hear the
grass singing to itself and the trees in the park murmuring in deep, sleepy voices. She could hear dandelions roaring and weeds pushing up out of cracks
in the city pavement, and she could hear the slow
voice of the sea saying "Old! Old! Old!" as it fell on
the beach at the edge of town. Everything that was
green Minnie could hear with her green ear.

Other Bullseye Books you will enjoy

Among the Dolls by William Sleator
Into the Dream by William Sleator
My Sister, the Vampire by Nancy Garden
The Ogre Downstairs by Diana Wynne Jones
Shadows by Lynn Hall

THE GIRL
WITH THE
GREEN EAR

Stories About Magic in Nature

by
Margaret Mahy

illustrated by Shirley Hughes

BULLSEYE BOOKS · ALFRED A. KNOPF
NEW YORK

TO JACK . . . keep on reading!

—M. M.

Contents

THE GIRL
WITH THE
GREEN EAR

Stories About Magic in Nature

The Good Wizard of the Forest

THERE was once a wizard who thought he was wicked. Everyone else thought he was wicked too, but he wasn't really. It was just that his magic used to go wrong.

He wasn't a very *good* wizard.

However, though he wasn't a good wizard, he was a remarkable cook. He made wonderful chocolate cakes with ten eggs beaten into them and melted chocolate poured on top. He wanted to give a chocolate cake party and invite all the children in town. He sent out invitations for tea and chocolate cake on special party cards, but nobody came. The children thought he was wicked. They thought he would turn them into creepy-crawlies. They did not know he could make wonderful chocolate cakes, so they stayed at home.

He had no pets and no friends.

Then one day he found a seedling tree—a little scraggly apple tree trying to grow among some stones.

A tree might be company, thought the wizard, though trees don't really appreciate chocolate cake. He dug it up, took it home with him, and planted it by his back door.

"But you needn't think I'm going to spoil you just because I've adopted you," said the wizard severely. "I'm not going to waste a lot of time watering you and hoeing around you."

The tree wilted.

"Oh, all right!" snapped the wizard. "Just a bit of water, then!"

He bought a special red watering can and sprinkled the hot summer earth beside the tree. The tree grew and stretched out green arms to the sun.

The wizard stared sadly over the summer fields, brown and gold, to the chimneys and roofs of the town.

"I wish someone would come and have morning tea with me," he said.

The tree rustled its new leaves. The wizard had an idea.

"Perhaps a smidgeon of plant food?" he said to it.

Just for fun he made a wonderful plant food cake. He made it of leaf mold and compost, with a pinch of nitrogen. He frosted it with lime. Then he put it on a beautiful plate, a plate with roses on it that he had won in a raffle. He put this plate on his best tea tray with the red watering can full of water beside it and carried it out to the tree. After this, on his second-best tray, he put a cup of tea and a big slice of chocolate cake.

The wizard and the tree had morning tea together in the sunshine.

"Shall I pour?" asked the wizard politely. He sprinkled the tree with water from the red watering can. Then he poured himself a cup of tea.

"Do try a slice of this cake," said the wizard. "I made it only this morning." He gave the tree a slice of the plant food cake, crumbling it around the tree roots.

Then he took a mouthful of chocolate cake. "Oh, good . . . chocolate cake! My favorite!" said the wizard, pretending it was a great surprise.

Ever after this, the wizard and the tree had morning and afternoon tea together. When the wizard made himself a chocolate cake, he made a plant food cake for the tree. It kept him busy, and he stopped being quite so lonely.

"I wonder if trees get lonely for other trees," the

wizard pondered. "How about a bit of leafy company?"

He began collecting more trees and planting them around his door. This meant making more plant food cakes. The wizard carried a slice to each tree every morning, but his very first tree, his apple tree, was the one he always sat with and talked to.

The trees grew taller and taller. The wizard's house came to be filled with green shadows and golden splishsplashes of sunlight. Through his dreams the rustling of leaves ran like whispered music.

Even when he woke up in the morning the music went on. When he walked or ran it was as if he moved in tune to the steps of a secret dance.

Time went by. The wizard planted more and more trees. Other wizards forgot him, and the witches did not invite him to their sprightly midnight soup-and-spell parties.

One day after many years this wizard was sitting under his great old apple tree eating chocolate cake.

"May I offer you a slice?" he said to it, polite as ever. "May I pour you a cup?"

He crumpled plant food cake around its roots and sprinkled it with water from his battered old red watering can.

Suddenly voices came to his ears, voices like clear chattering water. Out through the trees came a group of children in bright summery clothes.

The wizard stared at them and thought he knew them.

"Is that you, Billy Borage?" he asked. "Is that you, Sorrel Silk?"

"Billy Borage was my grandfather," said the boy. "But I'm Billy too."

"Sorrel Silk was my great-aunt," said the little girl, "but I'm named after her."

"Are you the good wizard of the wood?" asked another child.

"*What* wood?" asked the wizard, puzzled.

"*This* wood, silly," said Sorrel gently.

The wizard stared around him. The brown and

golden fields had all disappeared. Trees and trees and trees grew strong and branching everywhere. He could not see the end of them.

"How time flies," he murmured softly to himself. He turned to the children.

"This isn't a wood!" he told them. "These are just my trees and I am a wicked wizard, not a good one."

A strange rustling sound swept through the forest.

"The trees are laughing!" cried the wizard, who

knew by now when trees laughed and also when they wept. "Have I planted a forest by accident? Have I turned into a good wizard without noticing? I don't feel bad, but then I never did."

"We found some old invitations in the town museum," said Billy. "They were in a drawer marked 'Very Dangerous,' but the cards were so pretty we thought they could not be really wicked."

"Only a *good* wizard would bother to plant a forest," said Sorrel. "So we thought we'd come to see . . . to see—"

"If you had any chocolate cake left," cried all the other children, laughing.

"There's always chocolate cake," said the wizard joyfully. "Climb up into the tree. Eat apples while you wait. I'll just cut the chocolate cake up into slices. Do you like small slices or big ones?"

"Big ones!" shouted all the children.

"That's funny!" said the wizard. "So do I."

The trees rustled and the children sang. The wizard cut his big chocolate cake into big slices. The party was happening at last. Trees were company for trees. People were company for people. Trees were company for people and people were company for trees.

Nobody was lonely.

And there was plenty of cake for everyone, everyone laughing and everyone leafy.

So *that* was all right.

The Girl with
the Green Ear

THE great conductor Garfield Fortune should have been a happy man. He had a good ear for music, as you could easily see, for his ears were shaped rather like violins. He could play not only the violin and the trombone but also knock out a good tune on the harmonica. Every night he put on a black coat and conducted the city orchestra until he was completely worn out and had to be sent home in a taxi. Other musicians gave him envious looks when they saw him on the street.

"What a successful man!" they sighed. "Not only has he got musical ears, but he also has a fine house so full of flourishing plants it looks like a tropical rain forest. And besides all that, he has a beautiful daughter called Minnie."

They did not know that Minnie was causing her father a lot of trouble. She was breaking his heart.

"You are breaking my heart," he said bitterly.

Garfield Fortune wanted Minnie to learn to play the French horn, but she tossed her golden curls and refused to do so. Some girls are like that. Whenever their fathers want them to do something (and all for their own good), they decide to do the opposite. It was natural that a man like Garfield Fortune should want his daughter to be musical, and the town orchestra badly needed someone to play the French horn. Their usual horn player, V. G. Sevenby, had entirely disappeared, and no one knew where to find him.

"The orchestra is not the same without a French horn!" cried Garfield Fortune. "Minnie, you could pick up the French horn in next to no time if only you would let me give you a lesson or two."

"But I don't want to be musical!" cried Minnie. "I want to lead a strange, adventurous life. I want to do something different from you."

"I command you to take French horn lessons," shouted her angry father.

"No!" said Minnie boldly.

"You leave me no choice!" said Garfield Fortune coldly. "I shall have to disown you."

"The houseplants will turn yellow without me," Minnie declared.

"Go!" thundered her enraged father, "and never darken my doors again."

"Don't forget to water the plants," begged Minnie.

She went to her room and packed her toothbrush and her savings account book. Then she set off into the big city. Garfield Fortune had not been expecting such bravery in a girl with golden curls and forget-me-not blue eyes. However, he was too proud to change his mind.

Minnie walked up and down the big city until she came to a rather rough street called Cabbage Row. As she wandered along it, a notice in a window caught her eye.

BED-SITTING ROOM
SUITABLE RETIRED GENT
NO
PETS, CHILDREN
OR PARTIES
NO
MUSICAL PEOPLE
NO
FRENCH HORNS

The Girl with the Green Ear

Isn't it lucky that I don't play the French horn! Minnie thought triumphantly. This is the very place for me. She knocked loudly at the door. When the landlord came, Minnie could see at once by his sad eyes that he was a man with a secret sorrow. However, she did not try to find out what it was. She simply asked if he would rent his bed-sitting room to her, even though she was not a retired gent.

"But are you sure you are not musical?" he asked, looking at her suspiciously in the evening light. "You look as if you might be."

"Certainly not!" said Minnie proudly.

"Then the room is yours," he said. As he showed her to her room, Minnie couldn't help noticing that he had rather nice ears. They reminded her of something, but she couldn't think what it was.

Now that she was starting a new life, Minnie thought that she ought to look different in some way. I know, she decided at last. I must get my hair dyed green. My father will never recognize me with green hair.

Next to the Harp and Banjo Rental Service on the main street was a hairdressing salon—Mr. Plato's Hairstyles—where Minnie asked about having her hair dyed green.

"What a good idea!" said the hairdresser, Mr. Plato himself. "I have a new dye I am longing to try, but my clients are foolishly nervous and shy." Nevertheless, Mr. Plato was very careless for a man in charge of a powerful new dye. He kept talking to another hairdresser about what he was going to do during the weekend and did not notice the green dye running down into Minnie's left ear. At the end of an hour Minnie's hair was a beautiful bright green, and so was her ear, inside and outside. There was nothing that could be done about it, but luckily Minnie did not mind. Her father would never recognize her with a green ear as well as green hair. It was a perfect disguise.

Yet no sooner was she outside on the street than Minnie suddenly found she could hear all sorts of voices with her green ear, voices she could not hear with the ordinary pink one. She could hear the grass singing to itself and the trees in the park murmuring in deep, sleepy voices. She could hear dandelions roaring and weeds pushing up out of cracks in the city pavement, and she could hear the slow voice of the sea saying "Old! Old! Old!" as it fell on the beach at the edge of town. Everything that was green Minnie could hear with her green ear.

Close at hand a little voice was crying "Help! Help! Help!" very sadly, and another fierce voice was saying "Eat! Eat! Eat!"

"This needs looking into!" said Minnie, for she was a very brave girl.

Her green ear led her straight to a shop that specialized in houseplants. Most of the plants were looking well and growing well. Some were like fountains, and some were like lace, and some were like green beads strung on threads of gold.

As she came in through the door, one particular plant tried to grab her.

"You've got to watch that one!" said the plant shop

man with a merry laugh. "It is a rare carnivorous plant, fresh from the jungle."

"Do you mean it eats meat?" asked Minnie sternly.

"Only when it can get any," said the plant shop man, "but I have it firmly tied up. It had sausages for breakfast. I'm very kind to it."

But Minnie was not interested in the wicked carnivorous plant. She looked behind some tree ferns and found a poor little houseplant looking very sorry for itself.

"What is the meaning of this?" asked Minnie, pointing at it. "You should look after your plants better than this."

"Oh, that one just won't pull itself together," whined the plant shop man. "It won't try."

"It needs kindness and encouragement," Minnie told him.

"Oh, well, if you think you can do better than me, buy it and see for yourself," answered the heartless fellow with a mocking laugh.

"I will!" Minnie said, and she paid for the plant at once and carried it home with her. There she put it on the window sill, where it would have a good view of Cabbage Row.

The houseplant was grateful for its new home and the interesting view, but it had had a hard time at the plant shop, for the man had often forgotten to water it and the carnivorous plant had kept on whispering "Eat! Eat! Eat!" It promised Minnie that it would do its best to grow, but though it tried hard, it dreamed of caterpillars and dryness and woke up terrified.

Minnie watered it and spoke to it kindly. "When I was little and had bad dreams," she said, "my father would play to me on his violin. You need soothing watery music of some kind."

As she said this, she suddenly remembered the shop next to Mr. Plato's—the one called the Harp and Banjo Rental Service.

"Don't worry!" she said to the plant. "I have a plan. You'll be green and flourishing in next to no time."

The very next day Minnie came home from town with a large strange-shaped parcel. The landlord helped her carry it into her room.

"Are you sure you are not musical?" he asked, looking suspiciously at the parcel.

"Certainly not!" exclaimed Minnie. "This is a sort of medicine for an ailing houseplant."

Still, she waited until he had left the room before she opened it. Minnie had rented a large golden harp carved all over with ivy and singing angels. She had also borrowed a book entitled *Beautiful Harp Playing in Three Easy Lessons* from the public library. Minnie turned to page one.

"This looks quite easy," she said to the houseplant. "Harp music is like beautiful silver rain. It's like waterfalls on the moon."

"There is no water on the moon," said the plant. (Plants know things like that by instinct. They don't need telescopes or astronomy books.)

"Well, if there *were* waterfalls on the moon, they would sound like harp music," Minnie said. She began to play at once, making a few mistakes, but not very many considering she had never laid a hand on a harp in her life. She got to page two in double-quick time.

There was a knock at the door. It was the landlord.

"I'm sorry!" he said. "You know the rules. No music."

"Don't jump to conclusions," said Minnie. "This isn't real music. This is a houseplant cure. This poor little plant has been having nightmares, and I am trying to help it." The landlord apologized for his mistake. He really did have rather nice ears. Minnie realized that they reminded her of French horns. They had the same neat, curly look.

"Go on curing the houseplant," he said. "I will bring you a soothing herbal tea and a plain biscuit."

Minnie went on to page three. How beautiful she looked, her green curls contrasting vividly with the golden harp, her green ear standing out against the rest of her pearly skin. She ran her graceful fingers over the strings, and wonderful sounds fell through the air like silver needles. As it listened, the houseplant relaxed and actually put out a new leaf.

The landlord brought her supper and sat listening to the lovely music, sipping his cup of herbal tea very quietly so as not to disturb her.

"That's enough for tonight," Minnie said. "Lesson two tomorrow."

The next day Minnie got up early and put her head (with its green ear) out the window of the bed-sitting

room in number 7B. All over the city she could hear the voices of ailing houseplants grumbling to themselves.

"I have mapped out a career for myself," Minnie told her own houseplant, and put a poster in her window. She also put a large advertisement in the paper.

The poster and the advertisement said the same thing. This is what they said:

> If your houseplant's had a fright,
>   I'm the one to put it right!
> If your houseplant's getting worse,
>   I will be a loving nurse.
> Rush sick houseplants round to me—
>   To Cabbage Row at 7B.

"I wish I had a gift for poetry," said the landlord wistfully.

"Caring for others brings out the best in us," said Minnie modestly, looking admiringly at the landlord's neat, curling ears. She couldn't help wondering about them—they looked so musical.

By lunchtime a small line had formed. Anxious houseplant owners had rushed their ailing plants over for kindly advice. With her green ear Minnie was able to hear what the plants had to say and was able to tell people exactly what the plants needed.

"Too much sun," she said. Or, "Not enough sun!" Or, "This plant needs a steamy atmosphere. Put it in the bathroom and take a hot bath three times a day."

Severe cases were left overnight, and Minnie played the harp to them. She got through lesson two and then lesson three. Sometimes the plants joined in in little green voices that only Minnie could hear.

One evening about a week after she had arrived the landlord came into her room holding a yellow book.

"Look," he said in a casual voice. "Look what I

found upstairs when I was cleaning out the attic."

The book was called, to Minnie's astonishment, *A Thousand Duets for Harp and French Horn.*

"Isn't that strange?" gasped Minnie. "If only you had a French horn, you could learn to play it, and we could make lovely music together."

"Just by a strange coincidence I find I do have a French horn in the attic," said the landlord. "I think I could easily learn to knock out a tune on it."

"You aren't musical yourself by any chance, are you?" asked Minnie sternly, for she thought she had had enough of musical people when she was living with her father.

"No! No!" cried the landlord. "Perish the thought!"

"Very well, Virgil," said Minnie (for that was the landlord's name), "we will try these duets, but for medicinal reasons only. I am sure they will suit my houseplants down to the ground."

That very evening, wonderful French horn and harp duets were heard on Cabbage Row, and a crowd collected outside 7B, listening with rapture. Minnie's bed-sitting room was soon full of plants growing so tall and green that it was rather like being in a tropical rain forest.

Meanwhile, over on the other side of the city, Garfield Fortune was a dejected man. Firstly, he was missing Minnie, for now there was no one to argue with, and secondly, the town orchestra was not doing at all well. People came to listen, but sometimes they would grow impatient and shout "Where's your French horn, eh?" and "What about a harp, then?" and other critical comments. These were sensitive music lovers who did not wish to hear Mozart's Horn Concerto played on a trombone.

Not only that, but all the plants in Garfield's house had turned yellow. There was no fun in sipping his evening sherry among a lot of yellowing vegetation. He picked up the evening paper, hoping that the usual bad news would make him feel better about his own miseries, and there before him was a big advertisement.

> Rush sick houseplants round to me—
> To Cabbage Row at 7B.

Perhaps I could get this plant expert to make a house call, he thought. Cabbage Row is a very rough part of town. There are no musical people in Cabbage Row, and they all have cauliflower ears.

Unfortunately, though, there was no phone number.

Meanwhile, Minnie was getting many commissions. She now had the job of looking after plants in the library, the bank, the town hall, and many leading restaurants. Not only that, she was asked to lecture on houseplant restoration at the university. In spite of her fame, the times she enjoyed most were when she and Virgil played their duets to frail plants in the evening at 7B Cabbage Row. They were up to duet number fifty-seven.

However, one evening their duet was interrupted. A police van passed down the street with a tall policeman leaning out the window and shouting through a megaphone, "Attention! Attention! A fierce carnivorous houseplant has broken its chains and smashed down the door of the Pot Luck Potted Plant Shop. It was last seen making for Cabbage Row. All residents are advised to hide under their beds. Do not panic! If you hear screams, simply put your fingers in your ears and count to five thousand. This plant is savage—repeat, *savage*—and should not be approached."

"I certainly won't panic," said Minnie, smiling at the mere thought. "Music hath powers to soothe the savage breast, and if that carnivorous plant should burst in here, we will give it a quick burst of duet number forty-two."

"How brave you are!" exclaimed Virgil, staring at her adoringly and looking very musical in spite of himself. "A while ago life seemed empty of meaning. I had nothing to look forward to except getting a bit of rent every so often, but now—"

"Oh!" cried the houseplant on the window sill (Minnie's first plant, now fine and vigorous, with many leaves), "a stranger in a cloak is coming down Cabbage Row."

"Does he look like a carnivorous houseplant in disguise?" asked Minnie.

"No—he looks more like a sculptor or an artist or a famous conductor," said the perceptive plant.

But at that very moment Minnie, with her green ear, heard a well-remembered voice saying, "Eat! Eat! Eat!"

"Warn him!" she shouted. "The carnivorous

houseplant is lurking in the shadows. Virgil! Play *The Retreat* on your horn."

Too late! There came a scream from the street below. The carnivorous houseplant, grown to monstrous dimensions on a diet of sausages, leaped out of hiding and wrapped its tendrils around the distinguished stranger. Bracing itself by curling its thick roots around a telephone pole, the plant prepared to devour him.

But Minnie flung the window open wide.

"Virgil—duet forty-two!" she cried, and a moment later a wonderful melody flooded out into the street. Up and down Cabbage Row, people who had been preparing to follow the instructions of the police and were about to fill their ears with cotton balls and climb under their beds came out and began to listen instead. The horn was like a wonderful golden vine twining through the air, while the harp was like silver cobwebs, catching drops of a delicate rain and holding them like pearls. Fortunately the carnivorous plant was distracted. It appeared to stop and listen intently. Virgil and Minnie played like people inspired. The music flooded the street with feelings full of forgiveness and hope for better things to come. Even the victim, desperate though he was, was deeply affected. His arms twitched, just as if he were trying to conduct, despite the deadly embrace of a carnivorous plant. The music changed. It grew more powerful and reproachful, filled with grief for the wickedness of the world. People wept, and the houseplant was deeply affected too. It opened great scarlet flowers, and tears of honey dripped from

24

them, showing plainly that the plant was stricken with remorse. Slowly its tendrils relaxed.

"How wicked I have been," Minnie heard it say, "going around saying 'Eat! Eat! Eat!' instead of giving my mind to nobler things." Though only Minnie could hear it, anyone in Cabbage Row could see that it was sorry for what it had done. It not only released its victim, but it also brushed him down and gave his hat back to him.

"I forgive you," the victim said, "but I must find the players of that heavenly music. I must thank my rescuers. I came here to consult a houseplant expert, for my plants are suffering from yellowness, but I have found truly musical people in Cabbage Row." Closely followed by the erstwhile carnivorous houseplant, he ran up the steps and burst through the door of 7B. Then he stood like one pierced by sudden arrows.

"My daughter Miniver," he cried (for that was Minnie's full name), "and V. G. Sevenby, my missing French horn player! What are you doing in this tropical rain forest?"

"I live here," said Virgil. "My house is 7B and so am I. I have recovered my powers of French horn playing, thanks to the inspiration of your lovely daughter, whom I now ask to marry me."

"Oh, Minnie, Minnie!" wailed her father. "How you have suffered! I see your hair has gone green with suffering. Never mind! Now that I have V. G. Sevenby back again, I forgive you. You can come home once more."

"No!" said Minnie. "Virgil can do as he likes, but I prefer it here. I am dedicated to looking after sick houseplants. I have a career, Father, and I shall not give it up."

How beautiful she looked tossing her green curls! With her green ear she could hear the houseplants cheering her on, and that helped her to cope with the look of deep disappointment that crossed her father's face.

"But you will marry me, darling Minnie, won't you?" pleaded Virgil Sevenby. "If you refuse, I shall never play the French horn again."

"Well, I might," said Minnie. "I'll think about it. After all, we are only up to duet fifty-seven. We have nine hundred and forty-three to go. We might get through them more quickly if we were married. Besides, I think I love you, and that makes all the difference."

Minnie and Virgil did get married. They started a new line of houseplants called the Sevenby Greens, and three times a week they played with Garfield Fortune's city orchestra, which was greatly improved by the addition of a harp and a French horn. As for the carnivorous houseplant, it became a reformed character and lived on soybeans, protein extract, and other herbal nourishment. Garfield Fortune's plants quickly recovered, and though Minnie's hair finally went back to being golden, her ear stayed bright green, and she was always able to hear the green voices of the world and secrets that nobody else knew.

The Girl with the Green Ear

It is safe to say that there was no town in all the world where there was better understanding between men and plants, and many people took to bringing their houseplants to the evening concerts so they could listen together to the golden tones of the French horn or the music of the harp sifting through the air like the soft silver rain of a happy summer.

The Playground

JUST where the river curled out to meet the sea was the town playground, and next to the playground in a tall cream-colored house lived Linnet. Every day after school she stood for a while at her window watching the children over the fence and longing to run out and join them. She could hear the squeak-squeak of the swings going up and down, up and down all afternoon. She could see the children pumping their legs, pushing themselves up into the sky. She would think to herself, Yes, I'll go down now. I won't stop to think about it. I'll run out and take a turn on the slide. But then she would feel her hands getting hot and her stomach shivery, and she knew she was frightened again.

Jim, her brother, and Alison, her sister (who was

a year younger than Linnet), were not frightened of the playground. Alison could fly down the slide with her arms held wide, chuckling as she went. Jim would spin on the roundabout until he felt more like a top than a boy. Then he would jump off and roll over in the grass shouting with laughter. But when Linnet went on the slide, the smooth, shiny wood burned the backs of her legs, and she shot off the end so fast she tumbled over and made all the other children laugh. When she went on the roundabout the trees and the sky smudged into one another and she felt sick. Even the swings frightened her, and she held their chains so tightly that the links left red marks on her hands.

Why should I be so scared? she wondered. If only I could get onto the swing and swing without thinking about it, I'd be all right. Only babies fall off. I wouldn't mind being frightened of lions or wolves, but it is terrible to be frightened of swings and seesaws.

Then a strange thing happened. Linnet's mother forgot to pull the blind down one night. The window was open, and a little wind came in, smelling of the ropes and tar on the wharf and of the salt sea beyond. Linnet sighed in her sleep and turned over. Then the moon began to set lower in the sky. It found her window and looked in at her. Linnet woke up.

The moonlight made everything quite different and enchanted. The river was pale and smooth and its other bank, the sandspit around which it twisted to find the sea, was absolutely black. The playground, which was so noisy and crowded by day, was deserted. It looked strange because it was so still and because the red roundabout, the green slide, and the blue swings were all gray in the moonlight. It looked like the ghost of a playground or a faded clockwork toy waiting for daylight and happy children to wind it up and set it going again. Linnet heard the town clock strike faintly. Midnight. She thought some of the moon silver must have gotten into the clockworks because it sounded softer yet clearer than it did during the day. As she thought this, she was startled to see shadows flicker over the face of the moon. "Witches?" she wondered before she had time to tell herself that witches were only make-believe people. Of course it wasn't witches. It was a flock of birds flying inland from the sea.

They're going to land on the riverbank, she thought. How funny. I didn't know birds could fly at night. I suppose it is because it is such bright moonlight.

They landed and were lost from sight in a moment, but just as she began to look somewhere else, a new movement caught her eye and she looked back again. Out from under the trees fringing the riverbank, from the very place where the birds had landed, came children running, bouncing, and tumbling: their voices and laughter came to her, faint as chiming clock bells.

Linnet could see their bare feet shaking and crushing the grass, their wild, floating hair, and even their mischievous shining eyes. They swarmed all over the playground. The swings began to swing, the seesaws started their up and down, the roundabout began to spin. The children laughed and played and frolicked while Linnet watched them, longing more than ever before to run out and join in the fun. It wasn't that she was afraid of the playground this time—it was just that she was shy. So she had to be content to stare while all the time the swings swept back and forth loaded with the midnight children, and still more children crowded the roundabout, the seesaw, and the bars.

How long she watched Linnet could not say. She fell asleep watching and woke up with her cheek on the window sill. The morning playground was quite empty and was bright in its daytime colors once more.

Was it all dreams? wondered Linnet, blinking over breakfast. Will they come again tonight?

"Wake up, stupid," Alison called. "It's time to go. We'll be late for school."

All day Linnet wondered about the playground and the children playing there by moonlight. She seemed slower and quieter than ever. Jim and Alison teased her, calling her Old Dreamy, but Linnet did not tell them what dreams she had.

That night the moon woke Linnet once more, and she sat up in a flash, peering out anxiously to see if the midnight children were there. The playground, colorless and strange in its nightdress, was empty, but within a minute Linnet heard the beat of wings in the night. Yes, there were the birds coming in from the sea, landing under the trees, and almost at once there were the children, moonlit and laughing, running to the playground for their night games. Linnet leaned farther out her window to watch them, and one of them suddenly saw her and pointed at her. All the children came and stood staring over the fence at her. For a few seconds they just stayed like that, Linnet peering out at them and the midnight children, moon silver and smiling, looking back at her. Their hair, blown behind them by the wind, was as pale as sea foam. Their eyes were as dark and deep as sea caves and shone like stars.

Then the children began to beckon and wave and jump up and down with their arms half out to her. They began to skip and dance with delight. Linnet slid out of bed, climbed out the window and over the fence all in her nightgown. The midnight children crowded up to her, caught her, and whirled her away.

Linnet thought it was like dancing some strange dance. At one moment she was on the roundabout going around and around and giggling with the other children at the prickly, dizzy feeling it gave her, at the next she was sweeping in a follow-the-leader down the slide. Then someone took her hand and she was on the seesaw with a child before her and a child behind and three more on the other end.

Up went the seesaw.

"Oh, I'm flying!" cried Linnet. Down went the seesaw. Bump went Linnet, and she laughed at the unexpected bouncy jolt when the seesaw end hit the rubber tire beneath it. Then she was on the swing. She had never been so high before. It seemed to Linnet

that at any moment the swing was going to break free and fly off on its own, maybe to the land where the midnight children came from. The swing felt like a great black horse plunging through the night, like a tall ship tossing over the green waves.

"Oh," cried Linnet, "it's like having wings!" The children laughed with her, waved and smiled, and they swept around in their playground dance, but they didn't speak. Sometimes she heard them singing, but they were always too far away for her to hear the words.

When suddenly the midnight children left their games and started to run for the shadow of the trees, Linnet knew that for tonight at least she must go home as well, but she was too excited to feel sad. As she climbed through the window again, she heard the beat

of wings in the air and saw the birds flying back to the sea. She waved to them, but in the next moment they were quite gone, and she and the playground were alone again.

The next day when Alison and Jim set out for the playground Linnet said she was coming too. "Don't come to me if you fall off anything," said Jim scornfully.

Alison was kinder. "I'll help you on the roundabout," she said. "You hang on to me if you feel giddy."

"But I won't feel giddy!" Linnet said, and Alison stared at her, surprised to hear her so confident and happy. However, this was just the beginning of the surprises for Alison and Jim. Linnet went on the roundabout and sat there without hanging on at all. On the swing she went almost as high as the boys, and she sat on the seesaw with her arms folded.

"Gosh, Linnet's getting brave as anything over at the playground," said Jim at tea that night.

"I always knew she had it in her," said Daddy.

The next night and the next, Linnet climbed out her window and joined the beckoning children in the silver playground. During the day, these midnight hours seemed like enchanted dreams and not very real. All the same Linnet was happy and excited knowing she had a special secret all to herself. Her eyes sparkled, she laughed a lot, and she got braver and braver at the playground, until all the children stopped what they were doing to watch her.

"Gee, Mum," Alison said, "you should see Linnet. She goes higher on the swing than any of the boys—

much higher than Jim. Right up almost over the top."

"I hope you're careful, dear," her mother said.

"I'm all right," Linnet cried. "I'm not the least bit scared."

"Linnet used to be frightened as anything," Alison said, "but now she's braver than anybody else."

Linnet's heart swelled with pride. She could hardly wait until the moon and the tide brought her wonderful laughing nighttime companions. She wanted them to admire her and gasp at her as the other children did. They came as they had on other nights, and she scrambled over the fence to join them.

"Look at me!" she shouted, standing on the end of the seesaw and going up and down. The child on the other end laughed and stood up too, but on its hands, not on its feet. It stayed there, not tipping at all. Linnet slid away as soon as she could and ran over to the swings. She worked herself up higher and higher, until she thought she was lost among the stars far, far above the playground and the world, all on her own.

"Look at me," she called again. "Look at me."

But the child on the next swing smiled over its shoulder and went higher—just a little higher. Then Linnet lost her temper.

"It's cleverer for me," she shouted, "because I'm a real live child, but you—you're only a flock of birds."

Suddenly silence fell, the laughter died away, the singers stopped their songs. The swings swung lower, the roundabout turned slower, the seesaws stopped for a moment. Linnet saw all the children's pale faces turn toward her; then without a sound they began to run back to the shadow of the trees. Linnet felt cold with sadness. "Don't go," she called. "Please don't go." They did not seem to hear her.

"I'm sorry I said it," she cried after them, her voice sounding very small and thin in the moonlit silent playground. "I didn't mean it." But no—they would not stop, even though she pleaded "Don't go!" yet again. The playground was already empty, and she knew she couldn't follow her midnight children. For the last time she spoke to them.

"I'm sorry!" she whispered, and although it was only a whisper, they must have heard, because they answered her. Their voices and laughter drifted back happy and friendly, saying their own good-bye. The next morning she saw for the last time the birds flying back over the sea to the secret land they came from. Linnet stood alone and barefoot in the playground, the wind pulling at her nightgown. How still and empty it was now. She pushed at a swing and it moved, giving a sad little squeak that echoed all around. There was nothing for Linnet to do but go back to bed.

She was never afraid of the playground again and had lots and lots of happy days there laughing and chattering with her friends. Yet sometimes at night, when the moon rose and looked in at her window, she would wake up and look out at the playground just in case she should see the moon and the tide bringing her a flock of strange night-flying birds that would turn into children and call her out to play with them. But the playground was always empty. The shining midnight children, with their songs and laughter, were gone forever.

Chocolate
Porridge
(and who ate it)

ONE Friday afternoon Timothy's mother was cooking, cooking for the weekend.

Timothy's two big sisters, Pink and Sally, were allowed to help her, but Timothy had to go outside.

"The kitchen isn't big enough for everyone," said Timothy's mother.

"I want to cook too," he said, frowning and scuffling his red sneakers.

"Boys don't cook!" said Sally.

"Boys can't cook," said Pink.

Timothy was filled with giant indignation.

"Some boys cook!" he cried. "John's big brother got first prize for gingerbread at the flower show."

"It isn't just that you are a boy," Pink told him. "You are too small to be a cook."

"You are too little to be anything serious," said Sally. She smoothed her blue apron with smug pink hands.

Timothy had to go outside.

Outside on the terrace the sun was splashing the stones with hot gold. At the end of the terrace, against the wall, were the garden tools, the rake and the two hoes, the blunt spade and the pointed dibble.

There was the lawn mower waiting to clash its teeth in the grass. There was a row of flowerpots. Timothy's father was painting inside the toolshed, and all the tools were camping out on the terrace.

One big pottery bowl caught his eye. It looked like a mixing bowl. Timothy pulled it out into the middle of the terrace and looked at it. Where the garden had been newly dug, the earth was soft and fine. It reminded Timothy of grated chocolate.

He thought it looked delicious.

Digging at the edge with a trowel, Timothy put grated chocolate garden dirt into his pottery bowl. He rubbed his hands in it. "It's got to be fine," he said to himself. "They *like* it fine."

"What *are* you doing?" asked Sally in her bossiest voice. She had come out onto the terrace behind him. She put her hands on her hips and her head to one side like a grownup.

"I'm beginning to mix something," Timothy answered in a secret voice. He wouldn't look up at her.

"Mixing what?" she asked.

"Something!" Timothy answered. "I don't have to tell you."

He rubbed his hands in the chocolate dirt and felt very powerful.

A moment later he heard Sally's high voice in the kitchen saying, "Timothy thinks he is mixing something real that someone will like."

"I suppose it's just the same old mud pie," said Pink with a laugh.

"Now, girls—remember he is just a little boy," said their mother.

Timothy sneered to himself about all of them.

"They don't *know* what I'm making," he muttered. "It's going to be something good—something unusual—an unusual sort of porridge."

A nearby lemon tree had lawn clippings around its roots.

Timothy added a few trowelfuls of grass clippings to the pottery bowl. He rubbed them into the chocolate dirt until you could scarcely see them.

"Cooking, cooking, cooking!" sang Timothy to himself.

"Some cooking!" cried Pink in scorn. She had come to shake flour from her apron. "You're a mere mud-pie cook!"

"This isn't a mud pie," replied Timothy. "It is something special. It is chocolate porridge."

"Chocolate nothing!" said Pink. "It is a nothing! A big dirty nothing!"

Timothy let his mouth smile mysteriously at the corners.

"It *is* something," he said. "It is the famous chocolate porridge."

Pink went inside.

"He says he is making chocolate porridge," she said to Sally.

Timothy had followed her in.

"Could I have some salt?" he asked. "They like it salty."

"Who do?" asked Sally.

Timothy tried his mysterious smile again.

"I don't have to say," he replied, looking sideways away from her.

Timothy's mother gave him some salt in a plastic cup.

Timothy went out onto the terrace again.

Soon the white grains of salt were lost in the brown chocolate porridge.

"Now the water!" muttered Timothy.

He filled the watering can at the garden tap and sprinkled water into his chocolate dirt, grass clippings and salt mixture. He stirred it lightly with the garden trowel and then sprinkled again.

"Sprinkle and stir! Sprinkle and stir!" sang Timothy. "That's how they like it. Sprinkle and stir."

He stirred with the garden trowel.

There came a good cooking smell from the kitchen. It overflowed down the passage onto the terrace.

Timothy sniffed his own bowl with its earth and water and grass clippings and salt. It had a nice smell of its own, but it was a gardening smell, not an eating smell.

"They like it that way," he said, stirring a little bit more.

Timothy looked at his chocolate porridge. He liked its color. He even liked its smell. But he did not really want to eat it himself.

"Some people like it like this," he muttered, but he did not know what people. He thought hard, but he could not think of anyone who would enjoy his chocolate porridge.

There were quick, heavy steps around the side of the house. Timothy's father came onto the terrace.

"Thrown out, are you?" said his father, smiling. "You're lucky. There is a terrible mess in the kitchen. Women everywhere."

"I've been mixing too," said Timothy. "Look! I've made chocolate porridge."

His father looked at it. His eyebrows arched with surprise.

"So you have!" his father said. "My word, it's been years since I've seen chocolate porridge like that. It's very good. It's—I don't know how to put it—so fine, so well mixed. You've made a good job of it, I'd say. Do you think it needs just a little more water, perhaps?"

Timothy stirred and sprinkled.

"But Dad," he whispered, "who will eat it? Pink and Sally have been bossing all afternoon, and I said someone would eat the chocolate porridge, but now I can't think who would eat it."

"It just happens," said his father, "that today of all days I can help you. I've brought a permanent boarder home with me. This boarder is in the back of the car, and I think he will love that chocolate porridge. It is just what he needs. Let's go around the side of the house. No need to let the women know what we're up to."

The permanent boarder was taller than Timothy and had green leaves. It was a garden tree, an apple tree. It held out its branches like stiff little arms.

"Pleased to meet you," said Timothy, shaking hands.

"Chocolate porridge. I need chocolate porridge," sighed the apple tree, or Timothy thought it did.

Then Timothy and his father carried the apple tree to the garden, and while Timothy went to and fro collecting the spade and carrying the chocolate porridge and the watering can full of water, his father changed into his old trousers.

Together they dug a suitable hole. Then they untied the sacking from around the apple tree's roots. They put the tree into the hole, and Timothy was the one who spread the roots out and poured the chocolate porridge all over them.

The chocolate porridge made a very chocolaty-porridgy slapping sound as it fell around the apple tree's eager roots.

"Doesn't it sound delicious?" said Timothy's father. "It almost makes me wish I were an apple tree."

Then they filled the hole in. Timothy, having had a lot of practice, was allowed to sprinkle with the watering can. His father trod the earth down around the apple tree's trunk. They drove a garden stake in

beside the tree and tied it so that the tree could lean on it if the wind blew.

They had just finished when Timothy's mother and Pink and Sally came down the path and looked over the hedge.

"Oh, wonderful! An apple tree!" said Timothy's mother.

"Yes," said Timothy, "and what do you think it's eating right now at this very exact moment?"

"I don't know," said his mother.

"Its roots are sucking up chocolate porridge!" cried Timothy in great triumph. "Trees love chocolate porridge."

Pink and Sally looked at each other.

"Just think—salty apples," said Pink, grinning.

"I didn't think of a cooking day for trees," said Sally. "It would be fun."

"Next time we'll swap over," said Timothy's father. "The girls can help in the garden."

"And Timothy can learn to cook scones," said Timothy's mother.

When they went in for tea, Sally's biscuits were rather pale, and Pink's biscuits were rather dark. But out in the garden the apple tree thought Timothy's chocolate porridge was just right.

The Trees

Ever since Elizabeth could remember, pine trees had grown along the north fence like a line of giant green soldiers marching down the hill, but today, a bright shining blue and gold day, men were coming to cut them down.

Judith and Colin, who were both younger than Elizabeth, teased her at breakfast-time. They were looking forward to the tree men coming with their axes and saws and they could not understand why Elizabeth was not excited too. The funny thing was, Elizabeth could not explain it to them.

"The trees will just *crash* down!" Colin cried. "Like bowling pins knocked over. Don't you even want to hear them crash?"

"I'll hate it!" Elizabeth cried. She felt as if every hair on her head were standing on end with anger.

"Why don't you want to hear it?" asked Judith, looking at Elizabeth with a round solemn face like a freckled owl.

"I just don't!" Elizabeth muttered. She wanted to tell Judith that she loved the tall green pine trees. When she woke up in the morning and looked out her window, they were the first things she saw. Flying above

them, the magpies would toss and turn in the air, making their strange silvery yodeling sound like a music box gone wrong. When the moon crept over the sky at night, Elizabeth saw it through the branches of the pines, and that dark line of trees on the greeny-brown hillside was her first sight of home when she came back from town. Because she had climbed them so often, she felt as if she knew every branch and hollow of them by heart. They were all her friends, but the largest tree of all was her favorite because her swing hung from its lowest branch. Elizabeth had grown so tall that she had to tuck her feet under her when she was on the swing, but she still loved swinging. Sometimes she felt as if the swing might come off and fly away with her to some magic land. It seemed terrible to think that after today she would never again swing high up and see blue sky through a crisscross of branches and twigs and pine needles. Elizabeth wanted to explain this, but somehow she didn't know the right words, and even if she did, she felt that Colin and Judith would not understand them.

"Anyhow," Colin said, guessing her thoughts, "Daddy says he'll make a new swing for us like one in the park."

"It won't be the same," Elizabeth said scornfully. "It will just be a dead *swing*. The one on the pine tree is alive."

"You're silly!" Colin cried. "Whoever heard of a live swing."

Daddy looked at them crossly.

"Now, you children!" he exclaimed. "Stop that bickering and sniping. Elizabeth, *I'm* sorry the trees have to be cut down, too—they're seventy years old and were here when Grandfather was born. But they've grown too tall—they're just not safe so close to the house anymore. They've got to go. I'm not happy about it, but there you are!"

"Yes, Daddy," Elizabeth said, "I know that." And she tried to take no more notice of Colin and Judith, even when they whispered to each other, watching her closely.

"Crash go the pine trees!"

Inside Elizabeth said to herself, "It won't be like home ever again without the pine trees."

After breakfast the tree fellers arrived in a truck. The back of the truck was loaded with axes and ropes and lunchboxes. And in the middle of all these things was a winch with wire rope wound around it. There were three tree fellers, and they climbed out of the truck and shook hands with Elizabeth's father.

"Hello!" said the tallest man of the three, looking at Judith and Colin. "Have we got an audience?"

"They've been looking forward to it," said Daddy. "Whereas Elizabeth here wants us to keep the trees." The tall man smiled at Elizabeth. He had white teeth and a brown crinkled face, and he was wearing a blue shirt. Elizabeth liked him for a moment, then thought to herself that he was a tree killer and did not smile back.

"Will you chop the trees down with an axe?" asked Judith.

"No!" said the blue-shirt man. "We'll use a chain saw."

"Is that a saw to saw chains through?" Judith asked, but of course she was only five and didn't know much.

"Don't be silly!" said Colin. "It's a big saw with a motor on it, isn't it? You don't have to push and pull it—the motor drives it and makes it cut, doesn't it?"

"That's right," said the blue-shirt man. "I can see you know all about it. Now let's have a look at these sticks!"

"Sticks!" Colin yelled. "It's trees you've got to cut down—not sticks."

"We call the trees sticks," the blue-shirt man said. "It stops us from being too frightened of them. It's dangerous cutting down trees, you know. They try to fall on us, but we're too clever for them. We make them fall where we want them to."

Elizabeth followed them as they all set off together to look at the trees.

Sticks! she thought. What a name for lovely green trees! She watched with a mixed feeling of being interested and sad while the men fastened ropes to the first tree in the line. Then the blue-shirt man started up his chain saw. It roared like a lion until he cut into the tree with it. Then it screamed furiously and sawdust flew out around the head and shoulders of the blue-shirt man. First he cut a piece out of one side of the tree and then he moved around to the other side, where the chain saw screamed and the sawdust flew again. Then he stood back and shouted, "All right—give her a go."

The truck engine started up and moved forward by inches. The rope grew tight. Staring at the treetop, Elizabeth saw it move as if there were a wind in it—a wind that the other pine trees could not feel. Then it started to fall. Elizabeth held her breath. The tree fell slowly at first, then faster and faster, until it smashed onto the ground with a sound like crashing drums, thunder, and tearing sheets. Branches broke. Pine cones flew into the air like startled birds. Judith and Colin screamed with delight.

"Golly! What a crash!" yelled Colin.

"I thought it was scratching the sky down!" Judith cried. Elizabeth did not know what to say. It had been exciting to see the tree falling—to see that great tower of needles, cones, and branches coming down at her (though of course it hadn't landed anywhere near her). Yet now there was a gap in the line of trees like a tooth missing in a smile. She felt sad again.

The chain saw screamed and the truck engine rumbled. Neighbors came to stare. Tree after tree came tumbling down. They lay in a great tangled mass of broken branches and oozing pine gum, smelling of the gum and bruised pine needles. They weren't part of a grand row of trees anymore—they were just a mess.

Then it was lunchtime. The men got their lunchboxes and sat down to eat. Colin and Judith sat down beside them talking, while Elizabeth lurked a little ways off, not wanting to join in but not wanting to miss out on anything. Suddenly the blue-shirt man looked over Colin's head straight at her.

"You're quiet today, lassie," he said. "So you're sorry to lose the trees!" Before Elizabeth could reply, he went on. "Think it's sad m'self to see those sticks come down, but some of them are old and tired, really dangerous. And don't you go thinking you're losing out altogether. You're losing the trees, sure, but look at the view. We're not just cutting down trees for your dad—we're letting in the world."

Elizabeth looked at the view. Up till now she had just been seeing it as a space where pine trees had been growing. Now she realized she could see right across the valley from her own hillside to the great greeny-brown hills opposite. In between lay farms and fields and the winding line of the creek, with its fringe of poplars and willows. She could see the dark green shapes of the pine trees and firs and the small white shapes of the sheep with their shadows beside them, short and stumpy because it was midday. Elizabeth had a feeling of space and sky she had never had before. Deep down inside her she knew that she would come to love this even more than she had loved her pine trees.

She looked at the blue-shirt man and smiled uncertainly.

During the afternoon, when more of the trees came down, Elizabeth looked at the widening space they left with a different feeling. She saw still more of the hills and the widening, wandering creek come out from behind the pine trees. The new view was like a butterfly struggling out of its chrysalis—something gained, not lost.

At last there was only the swing tree left. Elizabeth did not want to watch it fall. She went inside, but all the time her ears were listening for the crash. It did not come. Instead she heard the truck start up and go away. When she looked out the window she saw her new wide view, and at the very end of it a single green soldier stood on guard—the swing tree.

Out ran Elizabeth into the kitchen, where Colin and Judith were eating bread and jam. When Colin saw her, he said, "Anyhow, they didn't cut down your old swing tree, so there. It's still a strong tree and not anywhere near the house, so the man in the blue shirt asked Daddy and Daddy said to leave it."

"It was the biggest tree of all," said Judith, but Elizabeth scarcely heard her. She ran out into the yard. It was not easy to get to the swing tree now, for the back of the yard was filled with the fallen pines, but Elizabeth weaved her way over and under the gray trunks and branches. At last she stood under the old tree. She touched the swing dangling from it. She looked up at the sky through its branches and felt its rough bark under her hand.

"Hello!" she said softly. "Are you still here?" Then she got on the swing and worked her way up high, sweeping backward and forward in a long swooping line. Above her the pine tree rustled and whispered as if it were talking to her. As she swung there, she suddenly thought of the blue-shirt man and wished she had said thank you.

The Merry-go-round

THERE was once a fair traveling from town to town. Such a gay fair, with balloons and fortunetellers and cotton candy and peanuts; with monkeys, performing dogs, a fat lady, and a mermaid. You have probably seen lots of fairs like it.

But the prettiest thing of all in the fair was a merry-go-round with ten prancing horses. Each horse had a flowing mane and tail of real horsehair, a fine arching neck, and swift galloping hoofs. They went round and round under a roof painted with new moons, with comets, and with silver faraway stars, so that the children who rode on them could look up and imagine they were frisking at night into a dark blue and silver sky.

The two men who owned the merry-go-round were

58

called Todd and Barney. It was Todd who had carved the horses and made their proud, red-leather saddles, but it was Barney who started the motor and who oiled it and greased it and kept it purring softly. It needed to be very soft because once the motor was going steadily Barney would pick up his brown violin and play the merriest dancing music you ever heard, while Todd kept time with him, hitting little strips of metal with a special tiny hammer. It sounded like fairy music—a fiddle and gentle chiming bells heard on a summer day. And all the time the engine went *chug*, chug, chug, *chug*, chug, chug in the background, and the horses went round and round, bowing and rocking in a stately dance.

The trouble was that Barney and Todd were not good businessmen. When they saw that the children were enjoying their ride, Barney would wink and Todd would nod, and off the children would go for another three minutes without paying any extra. Then when the master of the fair came around at the end of the day, and Barney and Todd had to give him half the money they had earned—why, the master would pull a very long face and say, "Is that all?"

"That's all," Todd would say, looking uncomfortable.

"Have you been giving free rides again?" the master would ask.

"Just a few!" Barney would mutter. "But the children loved it."

Then the master would say, "When will you learn

that business is business? Free rides don't earn you your living." And he would stump off.

One day they came to quite a new town by a dark wood, and there the fair set itself up—peanuts, monkeys, mermaid, and all. Barney and Todd were there too. Off went the horses, off went Barney on the violin, and off went Todd with his hammer. As they played, Todd saw a little boy walk out of the wood and stand there watching them. His eyes were like deep brown pools in a creek.

When the music and the horse's dance ended, Todd said, "Would you like a ride, son?"

"I haven't got any money!" said the boy in a small, thin voice. Todd winked at Barney, and Barney nodded to Todd.

"Hop on son," said Todd, "and we'll give you a spin for nix." Which meant a free ride for the brown-eyed boy. Round and round he went, and his eyes glowed, and the brown horse he rode went in sweeping free bounds as if at any moment it might break free and fly over the wood on its own. After the ride the boy thanked them, and Todd saw him run back into the wood.

"That's a funny thing," he said to Barney. "He must live there."

"There's no law against that, is there?" asked Barney.

"No, but I wonder what it would be like to live in a wood," Todd said. "It might be a happy place to live."

"Or it might be wet!" said Barney, starting the engine up again.

The day went by just as you might expect for a merry-go-round at a fair, but that evening, just as Barney and Todd had finished packing their merry-go-round onto the back of their little green van, they heard a great noise and a roaring of wheels, and into the fair came a big truck, and on the sides of the truck was painted MERCURY MERRY-GO-ROUND LTD.

"Mercury Merry-go-round?" cried Barney. "What does this mean? Don't they know that this fair has a merry-go-round already?"

"I'll tell you what it means!" cried the fair master, suddenly popping up beside them. "It means the end of free rides, the end of violins and bells, the end of Barney and Todd and their ten prancing horses. You weren't earning enough money, so I sent for a new merry-go-round. Its horses swing out fierce and far, and it has fine loud music on a phonograph and loudspeakers. And its owner will never allow any free rides. He is a businessman. As for you, I don't want to see you or hear your miserable *chug*, chug, chug machine again. My word, you should hear how the engine of my new merry-go-round roars."

And roaring with noisy laughter, the fair master stumped away.

That evening, when the fair left town, it left behind it Barney and Todd, sadly sitting on the running board of their van.

Over the hill the moon rose round and bright, but

Barney and Todd still sat there. They had nowhere to go. Then beside them a shadow stirred. They turned around, and there was the boy from the wood. He was quite bare, except for a kilt of green and a garland of starry white flowers in his hair.

"Here, you should be in bed!" said Barney, startled. "What's you mother thinking of, letting you out this time of night?"

The boy fixed his bright eyes on them.

"Barney and Todd," he said, "there's more kinds of business in the world than making money. So take me into your van with you and drive where I tell you, and you won't lose by it."

"Here, there's something funny about this . . ." began Barney.

But Todd said, "Go on, Barney, be a sport. Maybe the kid's got a party on somewhere and we can liven it up a bit for him." So the three of them got into the van, and the boy directed them into the wood. It was not easy to drive there at night, yet Barney seemed to find it no trouble at all.

"It seems as if the trees are making way for me," he said.

"When you have one of the wood people with you," the boy replied, "all ways are open to you."

Then Barney and Todd looked at the boy and saw that he was indeed one of the wood people—people who live with the trees and moss and fern and hide from the eyes of the world.

"See what you've let us in for now," groaned Barney.

But Todd said, "Go on with you, maybe our luck's changing."

At last they arrived in a clear moonlit place surrounded by trees.

"Put up your merry-go-round here," the boy told them, "and we'll see what we shall see."

So there in the moonlight a strange scene took place. Barney and Todd set up their merry-go-round. Todd talked to the horses as he polished their saddles and combed their manes. Then Barney pulled the starter rope and off went the engine—*chug*, chug, chug, off went the horses, off went Barney on the violin, off went Todd on the bells. The black and silver glade was filled with the beat and melody of Barney and Todd's merry-go-round. As they played, both Barney and Todd first felt the gaze of many eyes on them and then saw a shadowy line forming as the wood people came out to watch and wonder. When Barney stopped the engine and the horses slowed down, these strange people, these midnight people, came forward and climbed silently onto the horses' backs. They didn't shout and laugh like the children, and Barney and Todd found it hard to see them. They caught the gleam of eyes and heard a sound like the wind in leaves, but nobody said anything to them, nobody questioned them.

All night Barney and Todd worked their merry-go-round in the moonlit glade, until they fell asleep in the early morning. When they woke up, the boy was standing there with a bowl of milk and a bowl of fruit.

"Stay and play for the wood people tonight," he said, "and you will go neither hungry nor thirsty."

Barney and Todd stayed in the wood for some time, sleeping during the day and working their merry-go-round at night for the shadowy wood people who came and went, saying not a please or a thank you.

"They're not what you'd call cheerful," grumbled Barney. "Not a laugh or a smile in the whole lot of them."

"I miss the kids and the fun of the fair," agreed Todd, "but there you are—it's a living, isn't it?"

Then one day their friend the boy came to them, bringing a big poster. "This was stuck on a telephone pole just outside of town," he said. "I thought you'd like to see it."

Barney and Todd stared at it. It read:

GREAT MERRY-GO-ROUND
COMPETITION

A merry-go-round competition will be held on the fairground. The winner will be given a thousand pounds and the title of the World's Most Wonderful Merry-go-round. All merry-go-rounds may enter.

Everybody come!

"It's today!" cried Todd. "Let's hurry, Barney. Thank you, Boy, for showing us this. We will come back and play for you tonight, but we would like to enter this grand merry-go-round contest."

"And so you shall," the boy said. "Look at your merry-go-round! While you slept the wood people painted it for you again and combed the manes and tails of your horses. Now we are going to teach you a tune to play. It will bring you good luck."

And the boy hummed a strange little song. Barney soon learned to play it on his violin, and Todd beat it

out with his hammer. All around they felt as if the people of the wood were listening and watching and wishing them luck.

"Do you know it now?" asked the boy. "Don't forget it, and off you go, and we wood people hope you will do well."

As they left the glade in their green van, Barney and Todd saw the air shine and sparkle as if it were full of fireflies. They heard a misty sound like the echo of pipes and bells. It was the first sound they had heard from the shadowy wood people. It was the wood people laughing. Barney and Todd looked out into the shine and the shadow and laughed too. Their laughing made its own sparkle in the soft dark under the trees. Probably no one else in the world had laughed and sparkled with the people of the wood.

Well, the fairground was crowded with merry-go-rounds of all sizes. But they were all bigger and gaudier and louder than the little merry-go-round of Barney and Todd. Ten children were chosen to judge the merry-go-rounds, and all day they went round and round and round, sometimes higher, sometimes faster, sometimes noisier, with rests in between because they were so giddy. At last in the evening they came to the little merry-go-round of Barney and Todd.

"Ha, ha, ha!" roared the other merry-go-round owners. "What a sight! They won't get much fun out of that one."

"Ho, ho, ho!" sniggered the fair owners. "I wouldn't have them on *my* fairgrounds."

But the children noticed the beautiful prancing horses and the wonderful colors that seemed to glow and shine. They climbed into the comfortable polished red-leather saddles. In the late afternoon light the eyes of the horses looked alive.

Then Barney pulled the starting rope. *Chug*, chug, chug—off went the engine, off went the horses, off went Barney on the violin, and off went Todd on the bells. They played the tune of the wood people.

Then out from the ears of the horses came blue and white butterflies in clouds, out from under the bow of Barney's violin came flocks of bluebirds and dragonflies. Up around the center of the merry-go-round grew leaves and grapes and white flowers, so that the children could reach out and pick them as they went past. The blue starry roof went up and up and spread all over the sky, and the new moon, comets, and stars frolicked together. And last of all, the ten horses grew rainbow-colored wings and flew up and up, to dance among the stars. When at last the tune came to an end, and the horses came back to earth and the butterflies, birds, grapes, and flowers vanished, the children got off and shouted that Barney and Todd had won first prize.

The Girl with the Green Ear

Now Barney and Todd were rich and famous, and all the fair owners wanted their merry-go-round to work for them. But:

"No!" said Barney.

"No!" said Todd.

They set off on their travels again with their thousand pounds. For half the year they go from town to town giving children free rides on their ten prancing horses, and for half the year they work at night in the woods of the world playing to the wood people, who come silently out of the shadows to listen and to ride.

And sometimes when the day is summery and blue or the wind is in the north or for no reason at all except that they feel like it, they play the tune of the wood people, and those are the most wonderful merry-go-round rides in the world. If you are lucky, you might have such a ride when Barney and Todd come to your town, and you need not pay anything except a smile, or a thank you, or a laugh, or a kiss.

Thunderstorms and Rainbows

THIS is a story about a town called Trickle—a babbling, bubbling, swishing, swashing, murmuring, meandering kind of a town. And in this town lived a lovely young policewoman named Geraldine Busby, the one representative of the law in Trickle. Geraldine had been born in Trickle, and she loved it dearly. She wanted travelers and tourists to enjoy its strange beauties too, but they practically always went over it or around it, because Trickle was a town with a problem.

Whenever relations visited people in the town of Trickle (which they did very reluctantly), they always put up their umbrellas and began by saying, "Goodness, it *does* rain here, doesn't it?" Which it certainly did. For Trickle was the rainiest town in the world.

The Girl with the Green Ear

There were a lot of good things about it that people could have mentioned. It had a wonderful drainage system, for instance, but somehow there aren't many people interested in drains. It was also the greatest manufacturing center for umbrellas in the whole country, from plain gentlemen's black to enormous umbrellas for families of ten, covered with lovely pictures of moons and stars or printed with cheerful jokes that you could read from underneath. The national galoshes championships were always held in Trickle, but this too somehow failed to catch the public interest. Even the municipal fountain was little known and appreciated, though it should have been famous. Most towns have fountains that shoot elegant sprays of water into the air, but in Trickle, where so much water was coming down already, the fountain shot fireworks, spinning Catherine wheels, soaring rockets, and big gold and green sparks that flew up like birds and then burst into showers of lights. The children of Trickle, watching from their windows, loved to see these lights fall away like fiery moths and then go out one by one. It was remarkable. It is only possible to have a fireworks fountain in a very damp town, you see. It is too dangerous in a dry one.

The sound of water was everywhere. It purred on the roofs and purled in the gutters. It sang in a thousand voices in the moats and canals and in the conduits and culverts that ran around Trickle. It dashed along ditches, grumbling to itself, and chuckled in channels, plinked off edges, plunked off points, and had so much to say for itself that no one could ever feel lonely in Trickle. Very few people in Trickle understood the water's mysterious flowing language, but one of them was Geraldine Busby, the police-woman.

Of course you couldn't grow vegetables in Trickle—except for watercress—but people had gardens all the same, filled with rushes and reeds and pink water lilies. And though there were very few cats to be seen in Trickle, there were many kind and affectionate frogs for the children to play with, as well as flotillas of white ducks with orange beaks, not to mention elegant herons and ibises. So there were plenty of pets to keep the people of Trickle company.

As for games, apart from swimming there was water tennis and water football and water hockey, and though the streets were seldom dry enough for bicycles, they were ideal for boats. Children went to school in canoes, mothers and fathers went to work in gondolas, yachts, punts, and rafts—whatever they enjoyed most.

But you know how people are. They always think the place where they happen to live is the best place in the world, and the people in Trickle were no exception. They wanted visitors to enjoy their town's water pleasures and to say how sorry they were to leave. But the polite ones always said, "Goodness, it *does* rain here, doesn't it!" and the rude ones said, "I can't wait to get out of this soggy, boggy, sopping, dripping, swampy, splashy puddle of a place," and went off on the ferry without even waving good-bye.

This made the Tricklers very bitter, and their town council passed a law forbidding visitors to make any remarks about the rain. It was the job of policewoman Geraldine Busby to wait on the wharf, and if any visitor getting off the ferry said, "Goodness, it *does* rain here, doesn't it?" she was to arrest them and put them in prison . . . the only floating prison in the world. It was built on a big raft, and during stormy weather prisoners sometimes felt seasick, though they were, in fact, about two or three miles from the sea. It was useless to try to tunnel out because the prison was guarded by specially trained eels, all eager to taste any prisoner who tried to escape. However, so few people came to Trickle that the prison was almost always empty in spite of this stern rule.

The Tricklers did their best to tell the world how enjoyable life was in Trickle. They had postcards printed showing the fireworks fountain and the pink water lilies, but though these were displayed in the best hotels and motels, no one seemed interested. There was never a great crowd of laughing vacationers with swimsuits and snorkels on the ferry that came once a week bringing ice cream, sausages, and other necessities of civilized life.

"If I don't get more customers than this," said the owner of the Merry Mermaid tavern, pouring out glasses of watercress wine for the local inhabitants, "I will have to close down."

Everyone looked very gloomy, because no town wishes to have its tavern close its doors, and not a sound could be heard except for the friendly purr of the rain on the roof and the song of a thousand little waterfalls.

Meanwhile, down on the wharf Geraldine Busby, in her policewoman's raincoat, was waiting for the ferry to come in.

"I do believe there's a traveler on board," she said to herself, and sure enough there was. Sitting among the ice cream and sausages was a young man with a pack on his back, eating an apple and looking at the wharf—and indeed the whole town of Trickle—with hopeful eyes, though what he was hoping for Geraldine could not begin to guess.

She watched him narrowly as he disembarked from the ferry.

"My goodness, it *does* rain here, doesn't it?" he said to Geraldine.

"I arrest you in the name of the law!" exclaimed Geraldine sternly, pointing to a notice stating that comments on the rain were punishable by a week in prison. He was the first tourist they had had in months, and it seemed a pity to put him in jail. But after all, the law is the law.

Still, Geraldine was sorry for him because he had looked so hopeful and because he had fair curly hair of a sort she particularly admired, and so for supper she took him a tray bearing a bottle of watercress wine and smoked trout. She even had some herself, though she sat on the other side of the bars, of course.

"But why should anyone object to rain?" asked the young man. "When I said, 'Goodness, it *does* rain here, doesn't it?' I meant it as praise. I love rain, and I was delighted to see so much of it because of my hobby."

"What is your hobby?" asked Geraldine, taking an interest in her prisoner as a good policewoman should.

"I collect thunderstorms," said the young man. "I travel around the world searching them out and observing them and storing them up in my memory. I never grow sick of thunderstorms. And as I came up to the wharf, I looked at your town and I thought, 'This is the place! I'll see a magnificent thunderstorm here, I'm sure of it.' But then you arrested me."

"The law is the law," replied Geraldine.

"Yes," agreed the young man, "and it's a pleasure to be arrested by a girl with curls as black as thunder and eyes like lightning."

"Talking of thunderstorms," Geraldine said, blush-

76

ing and changing the subject, "this *is* a wonderful place for thunderstorms. Thunderstorms and rainbows! There are lots of days when it's only drizzling, and the sun comes out and everything gets warm and misty. There are rainbows everywhere. Then suddenly everything darkens. Great black clouds roll in over the hills and stare down at us in between fingers of lightning."

"You have a lot of lightning, do you?" asked the young prisoner eagerly.

"So much that you can read a book by it. In fact lots of people rush off to the library during a thunderstorm," Geraldine said earnestly. "We get sheet lightning and fork lightning and a continuous roll of thunder—all boom and basso profundo, if you know what I mean."

"I know exactly what you mean," said the young man, "and I honor you for the beautiful way you describe it." He lifted his glass of watercress wine in a gallant toast to the lovely young policewoman.

"Well, I'm a bit of a poet in my spare time," Geraldine said bashfully.

"My name is Philip, you know," the young man said. (Geraldine *did* know, for she had had to write his name down when she arrested him.)

"I think that you have been telling people the wrong things about Trickle," Philip went on. "I've seen your postcards mentioning the fireworks fountain and the water lilies. Very nice, too, in their way . . . but they don't explain what it's really like here. Suppose you were to invite people to come especially *because* of the rain, and not in spite of it. After all, there are people

77

who travel great distances in order to find some sunshine, and since this is a world of opposites, there must be people who would travel a long way for rain."

"Do you really think so?" asked Geraldine, her eyes lighting up like lightning. "You think that instead of keeping quiet about just how much it rains here we should tell people boldly that rain is our main characteristic—our speciality, as it were?"

"I'm sure of it," said Philip warmly. "But we must get it all organized. Bring me some paint and paper and another bottle of that excellent watercress wine, and sit just there on the other side of the bars where I can see you. Somehow you seem to inspire me with your wonderful thunderstorm qualities."

Geraldine was glad to hear this. A policewoman likes to be of value to the community and to help prisoners adjust again to civilian life.

It was but a little while after Philip's arrest that a whole series of posters was sent out from the town of Trickle in the care of certain responsible citizens. These citizens traveled far, seeking out hot, dusty, and deserty places—places of constant sand and sunshine. And they stuck up their posters praising the town of Trickle.

WHEN DID YOU LAST SEE A RAINBOW? asked the posters boldly. COME TO TRICKLE—THE WORLD'S RAINBOW CENTER! And: TRAVEL TO TRICKLE AND TAKE IN A THUNDERSTORM. There were colorful pictures of rainbows and thunderstorms just to remind people what they looked like.

FAR AWAY, sitting on a baking-hot beach, was a rich man and his wife. Suddenly the rich man stiffened with profound interest.

"Look!" he said to his wife. "It's been years since I saw a thunderstorm." He stared wistfully at the poster.

"It's been years since I saw a rainbow," his wife agreed. "Shall we go in search of one?"

"Let's!" said the rich man, and they rushed off to buy a ticket to Trickle, followed by a lot of other people, almost as rich, who had not seen a thunderstorm or a rainbow for years and years, either.

Soon the first ferry-load of thunderstorm-and-rainbow tourists arrived in Trickle. Philip and Geraldine stood on the end of the wharf issuing them bright-colored galoshes and umbrellas printed with rainbows and flashes of lightning. The tourists were taken by gondola straight to the Merry Mermaid tavern, and while they waited for the thunderstorms to begin, they had a good view of the fireworks fountain and nibbled local delicacies . . . delicious smoked trout, smoked salmon, smoked oysters, delicate freshwater lobster, and of course lots of chips. The rich man and his wife were both very impressed by the fine flavor of the water-cress wine.

"We never expected anything like this in our wildest dreams," they said to each other.

Up over the hills loomed clouds of astonishing blackness. Across their swarthy surfaces lightning wrote its eerie lines.

"I'm sure it is a sort of electric poem," said the rich man, enchanted.

"Yes," said his wife, "and if we were quick enough we might read what was written there." She took his arm.

"We'll never be quick enough!" said the man in a curiously contented voice. "Some things are meant to be mysterious forever."

Like a great burst of applause for the lightning's mysterious never-to-be-read poetry, the thunder clapped its giant hands and sang among the hills. All the echoes joined in and so did the tourists, watching the thunderstorm from the Merry Mermaid tavern.

Then the clouds burst above them, the rain poured down, and water spoke in urgent chattering voices,

beating on the roofs, babbling along the gutters, quarreling with itself in the drainpipes, then rushing on gurgling and singing to join the mighty chorus of the magnificent Trickle drainage system. Lightning wrote again across the sky, thunder applauded, water gossiped and sang. Everyone was delighted—more than delighted—overwhelmed. The storm carried all before it. Then it passed. The rain grew quiet, and out between a break in the clouds the moon shone, painting every wet surface, every raindrop, with shining silver.

"Oh!" said everyone, and indeed there was nothing more to be said. They watched in silence, drinking their watercress wine, and then went up to bed. All had amazing dreams.

In the morning the sun was out, shining down through rain that was little more than a mist in the air.

"There it is," said the rich man's wife. "A rainbow!" A perfect rainbow stretched over the town of Trickle. "And a wedding, too," she added.

Out of the church a handsome couple walked—she with her black hair billowing like storm clouds, dressed in a gown of greeny blue that flowed and foamed around her and holding a bunch of pink water lilies and slender bulrushes; he, tall and handsome in his striped swimsuit. They came out of the church between two lines of policemen and policewomen wearing handsome official raincoats, holding bright umbrellas over them, forming a triumphal arch. Then they poled off toward their wedding breakfast in a gondola of the most romantic kind. A rainbow formed at the end of the arch, and tiny rainbows danced in the air like butterflies.

"My dear, this is a wonderful town," said the rich man's wife. "We must tell all our friends about it."

And later, when they had put on their own swimsuits and paddled in little canoes in and out of the pink water lilies, feeding the ducks and ibises and admiring the frogs that watched them out of round golden eyes, they said it all over again.

"We'll have to come back," they said.

ALTHOUGH the town of Trickle never became a great holiday center, people began to visit it particularly for its strange beauties. Boating people began to come too, for they could hire not only dinghies and canoes in Trickle but also gondolas, coracles, jolly boats, sampans, skiffs, punts, and various yachts. There was plenty for boating people to enjoy.

But Trickle's favorite tourists, the travelers that Trickle loved best, were the members of the Thunderstorm Fan Club and the Society of Rainbow Lovers. These two fine clubs had members from all over the world. Their members came to Trickle tired and weary but went away refreshed, for there is nothing more refreshing than a rainbow. And even if you never quite manage to read the electric poems lightning writes over the storm clouds, they are a reminder of the mystery and amazement of the world we live in—wet or dry.

Green Needles

ALL around Teddy's house marched the pine trees—more than a hundred of them. Although they were so tall and Teddy was so small, they often nodded at one another, and Teddy felt very friendly toward them. He liked their gray wrinkled skins and arms full of cones. He enjoyed the music the wind made in them, roaring like the sea.

One night one of the trees fell with a crash like thunder and the end of the world. Now Teddy had a wonderful new playground as he climbed up and down and around the fallen giant. He rode the springy branches as if they were wild tossing horses and then slid down into pine-scented shadows below. The tree became Teddy's house, all little green rooms and passages.

Then one day while he was playing in his house he pushed through a curtain of needles and found himself in a room he had never seen before. Someone else was there before him.

"Hello!" said Teddy.

"Hello!" said the someone else.

They liked each other straight away. The someone else had grayish hair and a brown crinkled-up face. He wore a jacket and trousers made out of pine needles, and his eyes were green, too, as green and sharp as the pine needles themselves.

"Are you a pine tree man?" asked Teddy.

"Well, I live here at present," the man answered. "It suits me because my name actually is Green Needles and we match, this tree and I. I am hiding from someone, so I have to match the place I hide in."

"Who are you hiding from?" Teddy asked.

"A very rich, powerful queen!" Green Needles said. "She is a bit too rich, really. I did some work for her once, and she wanted to keep me for forever. But no one can keep me for forever, because I don't care to be kept. Mine is a wild, free nature."

"What was the work you did?" Teddy wondered.

"It was sewing," Green Needles replied. Teddy thought he must mean *sowing* like sowing seeds in a garden, but Green Needles said he meant sewing with stitches and a needle.

"I can thread a needle with sunshine and sew gold, or with moonlight and sew silver. I can make my stitches with moss, or cobwebs, with the dust on fern

85

fronds and the feathers of a kingfisher," boasted Green
Needles, "but I must be free. So will you let me sit
here in this green room and hide until I am quite sure
it is safe for me to go out in the world again? Sooner
or later they will come and search for me here, and if
they don't find me they will go away and never come
back. I will be safe then. Will you hide me?"

"Of course I will," Teddy agreed, wondering who
would come looking for Green Needles, "and I will
visit you sometimes."

So that was what happened, and for several weeks
Green Needles sat in his pine tree room while Teddy
visited him and told him about the world. Then one
day Teddy's mother said to him, "I am going to visit
Mrs. Shaw and I'm taking the babies. Can you be a
good boy and look after the house while I am away?
I won't be long." And off she went.

Teddy was sitting in the kitchen eating a bread slice
with dates on it when the door opened. It wasn't his
mother at all. It was three strange people with long
solemn faces. One was a soldier, tall and glittering in
armor like fish scales. His black hair was braided with
red ribbon, and in his hand he carried a long slender
spear. At his side swung a sword in a golden sheath.
The second of the visitors was a woman as tall and
strong as a man, wearing a helmet crested with plumes
and a cloak of tiger skin over her armor. Her hair,
bright as a flame, fell down over the cloak to her waist,
and twisted in it were chains of silver and of roses. On
her shoulder sat the third person, a little old, old man,

so old he had shrunken back to child size. He was quite white. There was white in his clothes, in his face, and in his hair. Only his eyes were black, and in his hand he clasped a little black wand, which he pointed at Teddy.

"You!" he cried. "You, little boy! My wand tells me Green Needles has been here. Where is he?"

"He isn't here," Teddy answered quite truthfully, because Green Needles was nowhere near the house.

"A queen wants him," the old, old man went on, "a powerful queen. She will give you boxes of pearls and yards of crimson silk. She will give you the furs of wild white foxes. Where is Green Needles?"

"I don't know!" Teddy shook his head, and this time it was a little lie, because he knew quite well that Green Needles was sitting out in his secret piny room.

"The queen will give more," declared the old man, frowning at Teddy. "She will give fifteen baskets of scarlet roses and a music box that sings like a blackbird. She will give a box of silver lined with black velvet, holding a perfect diamond, and a box of gold holding a single dewdrop, and also a singing cricket in a cage of ivory."

"I would like a cricket," Teddy said, "but I don't know where Green Needles is."

"Lastly," said the old man, looking furious, "the queen will give to the boy who tells her where Green Needles is a chair of gold by her own chair at the table. That boy will walk beside her in the great parades, or ride beside her on a pony as white as snow, or sit beside her in her coach on a seat of midnight blue velvet, and be in all ways like a son to her."

"Well"—Teddy shook his head—"I don't know at all where Green Needles is."

"My wand tells me you are lying," the old man said.

"Your wand needs fixing," Teddy said firmly in answer.

Then the old man said angrily to his friends, "Search the house!"

They pushed past Teddy and marched into the kitchen. They pulled open the cupboards and flung the saucepans and the papers, the knives, the forks, the marmalade, the butter, and the good wholesome bread onto the floor. They went through the house slashing and searching. They tore books and the sitting room

carpet. The huge woman pulled the curtains down and tugged the drawers out of the desk. The soldier ripped the blankets off the beds and sliced the mattresses in two. Oh, it was dreadful to see how they searched— how they slit and split, chipped and chopped, hashed and gashed, wrenched, splintered, carved and quartered, and tore to tatters the poor old house. But they could not find Green Needles.

Then they went around and around the house and even searched the pine tree, but they did not find Green Needles in his secret room in the pine tree's heart. So at last they stopped.

"He isn't here!" said the large woman. "The magician's wand is wrong."

"My wand has never been wrong before," the old magician replied sulkily.

"This time it is wrong," the soldier grunted heavily, "or else Green Needles has a stronger magic than you."

"That miserable stitcher has no magic at all!" screamed the enraged magician. None of them took any notice of Teddy, who was standing nearby listening.

"Then your wand is wrong," the soldier sighed, "and we are wasting our time. Let us go and search some other world."

And they went off down the road, leaving Teddy to explain about the ruined house to his mother, who was just coming down the hill.

Teddy's mother was not at all pleased. She could not be cross with Teddy for so nobly and bravely helping his friend Green Needles, but it was plain that she wanted to be.

"Look at the place!" she cried over and over again. "Just look at it! What will your father say? He's bringing visitors home this evening, too. Look, they've even emptied out the vases. Oh, and the *inkwell!* They couldn't have thought your friend was hiding there."

But at that moment who should come in but Green Needles himself.

Teddy was amazed.

"You must hide!" he told Green Needles. "People are looking for you."

"Actually," Green Needles answered calmly, "I don't think they will come back. And so I can go on with my wanderings. I feel free again."

"I thought they would find you," Teddy said.

"Ah, but I sewed myself safely into the pine tree room and they went by me a thousand times, not guessing I was there. So you see I am safe, and so I will be on my way. But first, madam," he said with a bow to Teddy's mother, "I must help you."

"What can you do?" Teddy's mother asked, looking at the wreckage.

"Madam, I can sew!" said Green Needles. And he turned back his coat collar to show a row of green needles, some as thick as a big darning needle, others as fine as the feeler of an ant. From his pocket he took silks as many-colored as summertime.

Yes, Green Needles could sew like nobody ever sewed before. He sewed up the tears in the wall with butterflies and birds. He sewed up the tears in the carpet, and where his needle flashed primroses appeared with hyacinths, jonquils, crocuses, and the starry yarrow—all so real they seemed to nod in the wind. Teddy's mother didn't have a carpet anymore. She had a garden in every room, a garden you could walk over without bruising leaf or flower. The silks Green Needles sewed with smelled of rosemary and lavender and of pine trees.

Where the curtains had been slashed Green Needles mended them. Some he sewed with ivy, and among the leaves he put birds' nests with blue eggs in them. Thrushes and blackbirds peeped out into the room. Other curtains he sewed with spiders' webs, fine and silken, and with dragonflies and flag irises. He sewed the chairs with a mellow thread that looked like the rich shine in fine polished wood.

Then he looked at the ceiling, where the soldier's spear had poked and scarred.

"Now I shall thread my needle with sunshine," said Green Needles. He embroidered a laughing, jolly sun and a silver secret moon in the center of the ceiling, and around the edges he put the stars dancing in their beautiful patterns . . . the Ram, the Twins, Taurus the Bull, Capricorn the Goat, striding Orion, and the shy Seven Sisters—all the starry people shone over Teddy's head.

Then he sewed up the mattresses with stitches like a procession of ladybirds. Even the pages of the books he stitched together with tiny white and black threads, so that you couldn't tell where they had been torn.

Oh, Green Needles, Green Needles, there was never another like you—you were the greatest stitcher in the world.

Then Green Needles put his needles back into his coat collar and his silks back into his pocket.

"Now I can be on my way," he said, "for they won't come here anymore. They won't dare to admit I was hiding all the time and they missed me. If you knew what their queen was like, you would understand. A handsome woman, mind you, but sharp in the temper. They've gone off to search for me among the stars."

"Are you sure you won't stay a little longer?" asked Teddy's mother. "Stay for tea!"

"I don't think so," said Green Needles. "My inside tells me I need space and sunshine, the open road, and trees and flowers, stars and seas. In short, I need some wandering. The world gives me its colors and its shapes and its shadows, and they all come out in my sewing. That is how I give them back to the world."

So they thanked him and off he went, and Teddy never saw him again in all the world. But the flowery carpets, the sun and the stars on the ceiling, the butterflies and kingfishers on the walls—these remained as if the outside world had come into Teddy's house to keep him company and liked it so much it had decided to stay there. So after that, because he had helped Green Needles, Teddy walked sweet and saw gay, inside as well as out, for almost forever.

Don't Cut
the Lawn!

M R. POMEROY went to his seaside cottage for the holidays. The sea was
right, the sand was right, the sun was right, the salt
was right. But outside his cottage the lawn had grown
into a terrible tussocky tangle. Mr. Pomeroy decided
that he would have to cut it.

He got out his lawn mower, Snapping Jack.

"Now for some fun!" said Snapping Jack. "Things
have been very quiet lately. I've been wanting to get
at that grass for weeks and weeks."

Mr. Pomeroy began pushing the lawn mower, and
the grass flew up and out. However, he had gone only
a few steps when out of the tangly, tussocky jungle
flew a lark that cried:

> "Don't cut the lawn, don't cut the lawn!
> You will cut my little nestlings,
> which have just been born."

Mr. Pomeroy went to investigate, and there, sure enough, were four baby larks in a nest on the ground.

"No need to worry, madam!" cried Mr. Pomeroy to the anxious mother. "We will go around your nest and cut the lawn farther away."

So they went around the nest and started cutting the lawn farther away, with Snapping Jack snapping cheerfully. But at that moment out jumped a mother hare and cried:

> "Don't cut the lawn, don't cut the lawn!
> You will cut my little leveret,
> who has just been born."

Mr. Pomeroy went to investigate, and there, sure enough, was a little brown leveret, safe in his own little tussocky form.

"We'll have to go farther away to do our mowing," Mr. Pomeroy said to Snapping Jack. So they went farther away and Mr. Pomeroy said, "Now we'll really begin cutting this lawn."

"Right!" said Snapping Jack. "We'll have no mercy on it."

But they had only just begun to have no mercy on the lawn when a tabby cat leaped out of the tussocky tangle and mewed at them:

"Don't cut the lawn, don't cut the lawn!
You will cut my little kittens,
who have just been born."

Mr. Pomeroy went to investigate, and there, sure enough, were two stripy kittens in a little golden tussocky, tangly hollow.

"This place is more like a zoo than a lawn," grumbled Snapping Jack. "We'll go farther away this time, but you must promise to be hardhearted or the lawn will get the better of us."

"All right! If it happens again I'll be very hardhearted," promised Mr. Pomeroy.

They began to cut where the lawn was longest, lankiest, tangliest, and most terribly tough and tussocky.

"I'm not going to take any notice of any interruptions this time," Mr. Pomeroy said to himself firmly.

"We'll really get down to business," said Snapping Jack, beginning to champ with satisfaction.

Then something moved in the long, lank, tussocky tangle. Something slowly sat up and stared at them with jeweled eyes. It was a big mother dragon, as green as grass, as golden as a tussock, She looked at them and she hissed:

"Don't cut the lawn, don't cut the lawn!
You will cut my little dragon,
who has just been born."

There among the leathery scraps of the shell of the dragon's egg was a tiny dragon, as golden and glittering as a bejeweled evening bag. It blew out a tiny flame at them, just like a cigarette lighter.

"Isn't he clever for one so young!" exclaimed his loving mother. "Of course I can blow out a very big flame. I could burn all this lawn in one blast if I wanted to. I could easily scorch off your eyebrows."

"But that's against the law!" croaked the alarmed Mr. Pomeroy.

"Oh, I'm afraid that wouldn't stop me," said the dragon. "Not if I was upset about anything. And if you mowed my baby I'd be very upset. I'd probably breathe fire hot enough to melt a lawn mower!"

"What do *you* think?" Mr. Pomeroy asked Snapping Jack.

"Let's leave it until next week," said Snapping Jack hurriedly.

"We don't want to upset a loving mother, do we? Particularly one that breathes fire!"

So the lawn was left alone and Mr. Pomeroy sat on his veranda enjoying the sun, or swam in the sea enjoying the saltwater, and day by day he watched the cottage lawn grow more tussocky and more tangly. Then one day out of the tussocks and tangles flew four

baby larks that began learning how to soar and sing as larks do. And out of the tussocks and tangles came a little hare that frolicked and frisked as hares do. And out of the tussocks and tangles came two stripy kittens that pounced and bounced as kittens do. And *then* out of the tussocks and tangles came a little dragon with golden scales and eyes like stars, and it laid its shining head on Mr. Pomeroy's knee and told him some of the wonderful stories that only dragons know. Even Snapping Jack listened with interest.

"Fancy that!" he was heard to remark. "I'm glad I talked Mr. Pomeroy out of mowing the lawn. Who'd ever believe a tussocky, tangly lawn could be home to so many creatures. There's more to a lawn than mere grass, you know!"

And Mr. Pomeroy, the larks, the leveret, the kittens, and the little dragon all agreed with him.

Margaret Mahy

decided as a child that she wanted to be a writer. She is now the world-renowned author of over three dozen books for young people and the recipient of many awards, including Carnegie Medals for *The Haunting* and *The Changeover*. She lives in Governors Bay, New Zealand, and plans to write stories for a long time to come.

Shirley Hughes

grew up in Liverpool, England, and trained at the Liverpool Art School and the Ruskin School of Art in Oxford. The author-illustrator of over a dozen children's books and the illustrator of over 200 more, she has received many awards for her work, including the prestigious Kate Greenaway Medal for her illustrations in *Dogger*. Shirley Hughes and her husband live in London.

Little by little, they were drawn...

Into the Dream

by William Sleator

Every night it's the same dream—the strange one about the field, the big glowing thing, and the eerie figure in white. At first, Paul thinks it's just a recurring nightmare. But then he finds out that Francine, a girl in his class, is having it too. Realizing that it must mean something, Paul and Francine join forces and soon learn that the dream is really a child's desperate cry for help. Feeling the urgency, the two delve deeper and deeper into the dream. Can they find the mystery boy before their dream becomes terrifying reality?

"A thriller of top-notch quality." —*Booklist*

"A compelling fantasy written with increasing tempo and suspense."
—*The Bulletin of the Center for Children's Books*

A BULLSEYE BOOK PUBLISHED BY ALFRED A. KNOPF, INC.

Magical mayhem

The Ogre Downstairs

by Diana Wynne Jones

Caspar, Johnny, and Gwinny can't figure out what their mother sees in her new husband, Jack—they think he's an ogre. And their stepbrothers, Malcolm and Douglas, don't understand why their father took on such an obnoxious family. Then Jack gives each set of siblings a strange chemistry set, and the kids realize they've got bigger things to worry about. After all, these are no ordinary chemicals—they can make the kids fly, disappear, and even switch bodies. But is their magic powerful enough to keep this family from falling apart?

"An entertaining comic fantasy."

—*Washington Post Book World*

"Readers will be swept along to the end."

—*Booklist*

A BULLSEYE BOOK PUBLISHED BY ALFRED A. KNOPF, INC.